Is That an Elephant in My Fridge?

Written by
Caroline Crowe

Illustrated by
Claudia Ranucci

SCHOLASTIC

At bedtime, Fred was wide awake.
He sighed, "I just can't sleep!"

So Mummy tucked him in and said,
"The trick is COUNTING sheep."

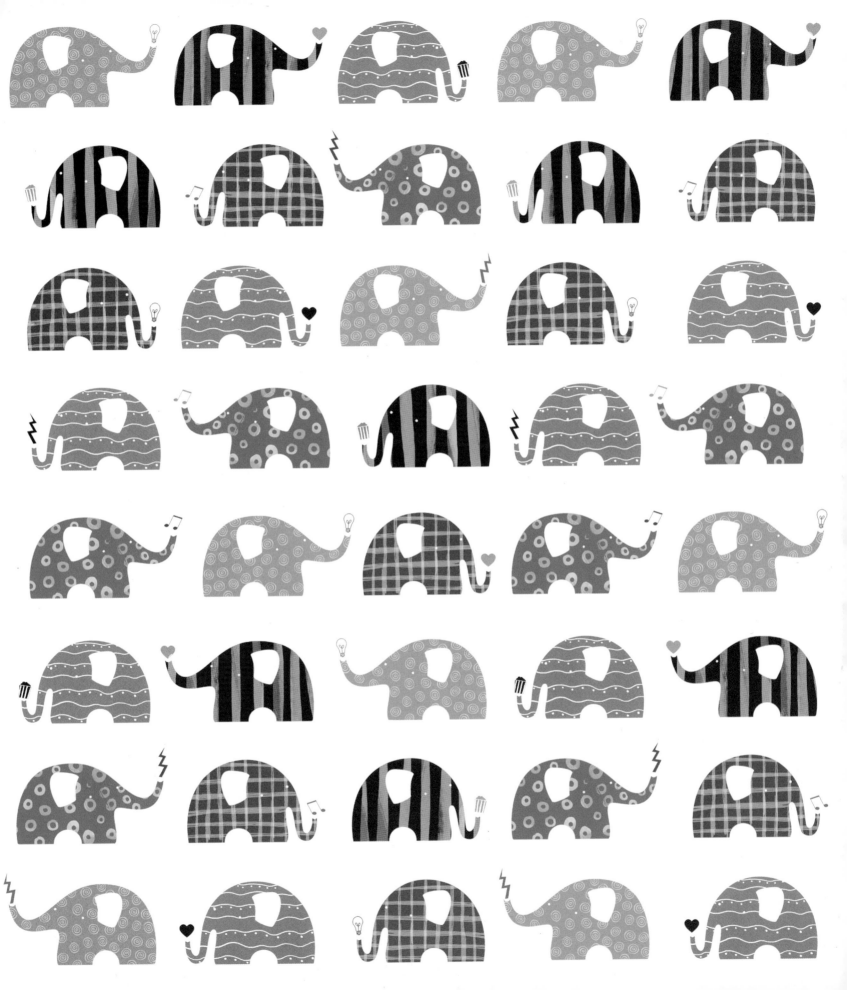

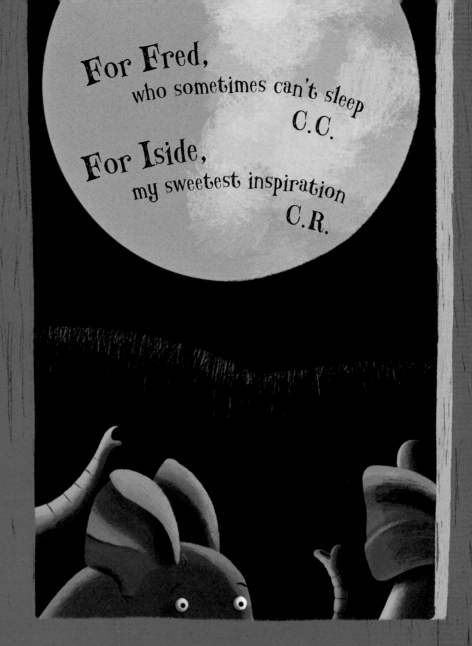

For Fred,
who sometimes can't sleep
C.C.

For Iside,
my sweetest inspiration
C.R.

First published in 2016
by Scholastic Children's Books
Euston House, 24 Eversholt Street, London NW1 1DB
a division of Scholastic Ltd
www.scholastic.co.uk
London ~ New York ~ Toronto ~ Sydney ~ Auckland ~ Mexico City ~ New Delhi ~ Hong Kong

Text copyright © 2016 Caroline Crowe • Illustrations copyright © 2016 Claudia Ranucci

This edition specially published for Scottish Book Trust in 2017
ISBN 978 1407 18495 1

But sheep, Fred thought,
are **boring**,
As he tossed and turned in bed.

So he closed his eyes and started...

...Counting elephants instead.

The first one had a **pirate hat**,
An eyepatch and a sword.
He was hunting round the toy box

for his **pirate treasure hoard.**

The second had a **cape** on
And some superhero tights.

He was **flying** round Fred's ceiling,

Trying not

to hit the lights.

Then Fred heard lots of **splashing**

From **more** elephants next door.

They were sitting in the bathtub,
Firing bubbles at the floor.

Three more were...

...on the landing,

Doing clever
circus tricks,

They were balanced on a beach ball,
While they juggled building bricks.

One wearing a **pink** tutu…

Did a **spin** across the floor,

And got wedged inside the door.

But she tripped on a banana,

Fred tried and tried to count them,

But the number grew and grew.

One flew past him on her scooter,

Was it one, or were there two?

Elephants were **everywhere**,

They'd turned the telly on,

One was **gobbling** ice cream,

And the
biscuits
had all gone!

On the stairs,
a marching band
Were climbing two by two,
When the leader
lost his footing,

With a trumpeting
ATCHoO!

He crashed

into the next one,

And the house began

to shake,

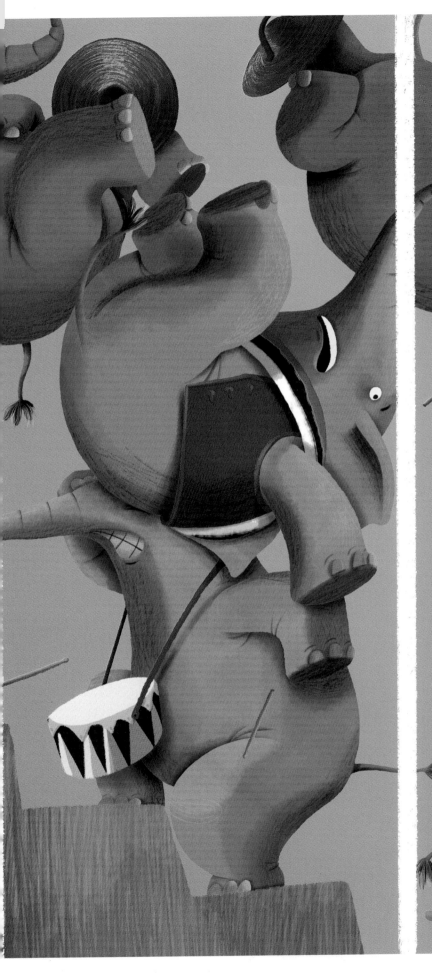
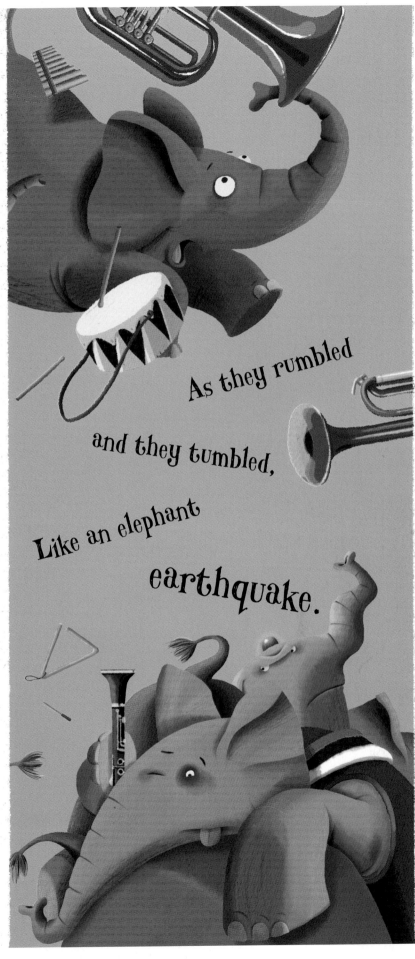

As they rumbled
and they tumbled,
Like an elephant
earthquake.

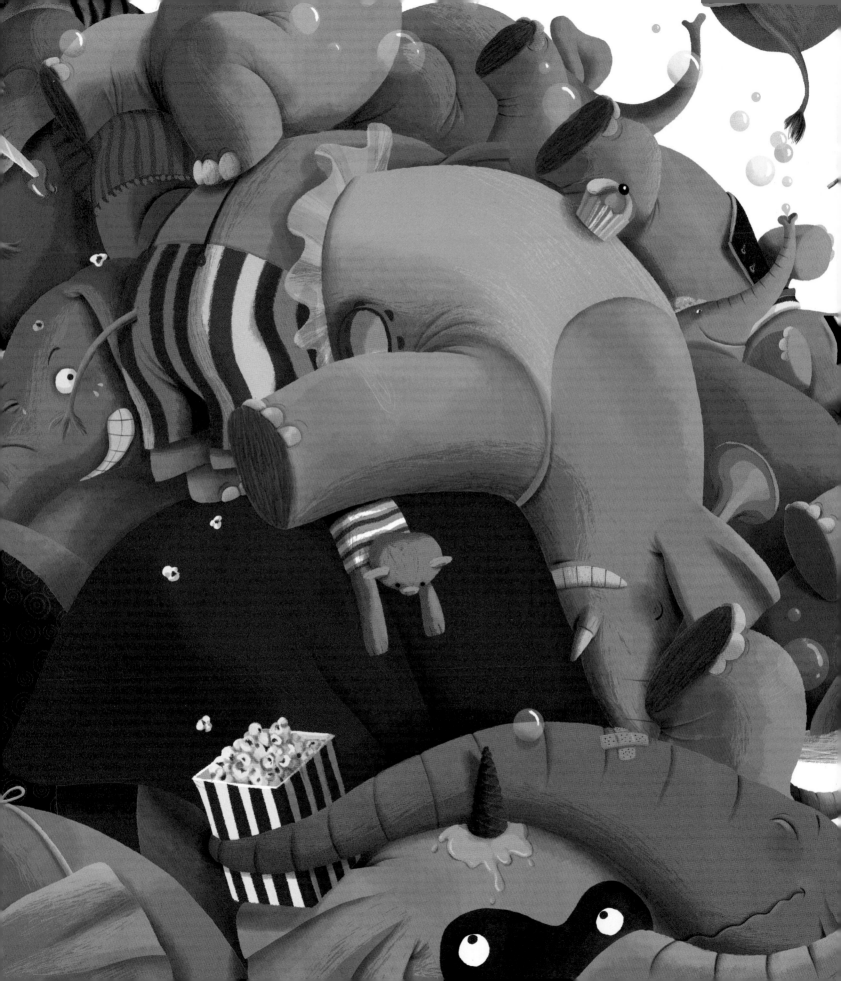

Their trunks were in a tangle, legs all waving in the air.

He'd never count how many were all jumbled up in there.

"Enough!" cried Fred.

"You have to go!"

He opened the front door,

Then he **crashed** a pair of **cymbals**

That were lying on the floor.

The elephants ignored him,
They were having **too** much fun.
Fred was out of good ideas...

...Then he had a **sneaky** one.

"Pack your trunks,
be **quick**," he said.

"Look, over there -
a **mouse**..."

The elephants
skedaddled,
They weren't staying
in **this** house.

"Phew!" Fred yawned.
He closed his eyes,
And drifted off to sleep.

"Those elephants were trouble –

I'll just stick to counting sheep."